BORIS
the Boring Boar

by Ellen Jackson
illustrated by Normand Chartier

Macmillan Publishing Company   New York
Maxwell Macmillan Canada   Toronto
Maxwell Macmillan International
New York   Oxford   Singapore   Sydney

E
JAC

c.1

For Cookie —E.J.
For Virginia, Matthew, and Baby C. —N.C.

Macmillan Publishing Company is part of the Maxwell Communica-
tion Group of Companies.

Macmillan Publishing Company
866 Third Avenue
New York, NY 10022

Maxwell Macmillan Canada, Inc.
1200 Eglinton Avenue East
Suite 200
Don Mills, Ontario M3C 3N1

FIRST EDITION
Printed in Hong Kong by South China Printing Company (1988) Ltd.
10 9 8 7 6 5 4 3 2 1

The text of this book is set in 16 pt. Horley Oldstyle.
The illustrations are rendered in watercolor.

Library of Congress Cataloging-in-Publication Data
Jackson, Ellen B.
Boris the boring boar / by Ellen Jackson ; illustrated by Normand
Chartier. — 1st ed.
p.   cm.
Summary: Boris bores all of his friends with endless chatter but
his nearly fatal encounter with a wolf teaches him the importance of
being a good listener.
ISBN 0-02-747662-6
[1. Self-perception—Fiction.   2. Wild boar—Fiction.]
I. Chartier, Normand, ill.   II. Title.
PZ7.J13247Bo   1992   [E]—dc20   90-48670

Once there was a boar who beat around the bush. He never said what he meant, and he never meant what he said. And he always talked about himself. He was quite a boring boar.

One day the boar, whose name was Boris, met a
raccoon.

"I say, Raccoon," said Boris. "That's a nice tin
can you have there. Tuna, isn't it? But they don't
make tin cans the way they used to. No indeed.
Why, I remember a tin of sardines I found in
'83. Or was it '84? No. It was '83. And it wasn't
sardines, it was soup. Campbell's, I believe.
Or was it spaghetti . . . ?"

"Oh, Boar. You're so boring!" said the raccoon.
And he hurried away.

"Well," said Boris. "The raccoons in these parts
are not at all friendly."

Another day Boris met a turtle.

"Mrs. Turtle, isn't it?" said Boris. "You're looking fit today, though a bit fat. I had an aunt one time who died of fat. Or was it an uncle? No, I believe it was a first cousin once removed. And she didn't die of fat, she fried a hat. Or perhaps she . . ."

"Oh, Boar," said the turtle. "You're so boring!"
And the turtle hurried away.

"Well," said Boris. "The turtles around here
aren't any friendlier than the raccoons."

Another day Boris met a sweet girl pig named
Pansy. Boris had often met Pansy while she was
gathering wild mushrooms in the woods. She was
plump and pretty, and had a lovely curly tail.

"Hello, Pansy," said Boris. "A plump, pretty pig such as you shouldn't live alone. Why I remember a pig I met in Bora Bora, or was it Walla Walla? No. It was Cucamonga. And actually, I think it was a pickle, not a pig . . ."

"Oh, Boris!" said Pansy with a little yawn. "You're so *boring*!" And she went on her way.

Boris was very sad. No one in this part of the woods seemed at all friendly. Why didn't other animals like to talk to him? He was lonely.

Suddenly, Boris saw a hairy stranger trotting
toward him. He would try once more.

"Hello there, stranger," said Boris. "My name is
Boris. Do you have time for a chat? I'm a boar, you
know, a lonely boar who would like to talk to
someone."

"Why certainly," said the hairy stranger. "I'd love to have a chomp . . . I mean, a chat, with you, Come closer."

Boris came closer.

The hairy stranger grabbed Boris and tied him to a tree.

"Ah! A plump juicy pig for supper," the stranger said, licking his chops.

"Why, you're a wolf!" said Boris.
"Indeed I am," said the hairy stranger.
He smiled, and his teeth gleamed brightly.
"Oh dear! Oh dear!" said Boris.

The wolf scurried around and gathered some wood. When he returned he built a fire and hung a big pot of water over it between three sticks. Then he sat down to wait for the water to boil.

Boris was very upset. Was this the end? Oh why, oh why was he so boring? Why, oh why did he only think and talk about himself? He hadn't even noticed that his new friend was a hungry wolf.

The wolf began to yawn. Boris looked at him. Maybe the wolf would go to sleep. Boring Boris was quite good at putting animals to sleep. But for once in his life, Boris couldn't think of a single boring thing to say. All he could think of to say was, *Help! Help!*

"I say there, Wolf, did you ever hear about the
Boar War . . . ?" Boris began. But then he stopped.
He couldn't remember anything about the Boar
War.

He tried again.

"Friend Wolf, do you know the difference
between a boar and a banana?"

"No," said the wolf.

But Boris couldn't remember the difference
between a boar and a banana.

The wolf got up to check the water.

"Almost ready," said the wolf.

Boris was so scared that for once in his life he had a clever thought.

"I say, Friend Wolf, you have a very nice set of teeth."

"Why, thank you," said the wolf as he added a pinch of salt to the water.

"And the way you do your fur is quite becoming. Do you blow-dry it?" asked Boris.

"Yes, I do," said the wolf. "Otherwise it stands on end and makes me look like a porcupine. When I was just a pup the other wolves would tease me about it."

"Were you from a large litter?" asked Boris.

"Oh, yes," said the wolf. And he began to talk about himself and his brothers and sisters and aunts and uncles and cousins.

"I miss the old wolf pack," said the wolf. "I get lonely in this part of the woods. And if I do meet someone new, I always feel I have to eat him up."

"It's hard to make new friends that way," agreed Boris.

"Yes, I do wish I didn't have to eat you," said the wolf. "You're interesting to talk to—for a boar."

Boris was surprised to hear that. He was starting to like the wolf.

"Why don't you change your diet?" said Boris. "It's good to try new foods now and then. Have you tried dandelion soup with wild mushrooms? I think you might like it. Then you could keep me for a friend."

"I might do that," said the wolf. "To tell you the truth, my mom and dad made me eat boark chops every day. I've never really liked them."

The wolf untied Boris.

"You'd better go quickly," said the wolf. "I shouldn't be seen talking to a boar. But come back when it's dark and we'll talk some more. I'll show you a picture of my uncle Wolfgang howling at the moon."

Boris scurried quickly through the woods. In front of him was a clearing, and there by an old gum tree was Pansy Pig, holding a basket full of wild mushrooms.

"Hello, Boris," said Pansy. "Why are you in such a hurry?"

Boris was very glad to see her.

"Oh, Pansy! Oh, Pansy!" said Boris. "I've had *such* a day! About three o'clock this afternoon I was walking in the woods . . . Or was it two o'clock . . . No, I think it was . . ."

Pansy began to yawn.

"Well, enough talk of me," said Boris. "How are
you Pansy? You're looking quite lovely. And you've
gathered so many mushrooms. I'll bet you could
tell me about all the best places to find them."

Pansy stopped yawning. She smiled at Boris.

"Why don't you come over to my house for a
bowl of dandelion soup?" she said.

Soon Pansy and Boris were seen rooting in the mud together every day. In the evening they were sometimes joined by a hairy stranger for soup and salad. Pansy and the wolf would talk far into the night about relatives and recipes while Boris listened.

And if Boris was sometimes a bit bored, he never let on.

DATE DUE
